This edition published by Parragon Inc. in 2015

Parragon Inc.
440 Park Avenue South, 13th Floor
New York, NY 10016
www.parragon.com

ISBN 978-1-4723-3137-3

Printed in China

Jack
and the
Beanstalk

Retold by Ronne Randall
Illustrated by Gavin Scott

Bath • New York • Cologne • Melbourne • Delhi
Hong Kong • Shenzhen • Singapore • Amsterdam

Once there was a boy named Jack who lived with his mother. They were very poor and had to sell their cow to get money for food.

As he was taking the cow to market, Jack met an old man.

"You won't get much money for such an old cow," he told Jack, "but I can give you something better than money for her—magic beans!"

He held out his hand and showed Jack five speckled beans.

Magic beans! thought Jack. **They sound exciting!**

He gave the old man the cow and took the beans, thanking the man politely. Then he went home to his mother.

Jack's mother was extremely cross.

"Silly boy!" she shouted.

"Thanks to you,
we have no cow
and no money!"

She threw the beans out of the
window and sent Jack straight to bed.

The next morning, Jack was astonished when he looked out of the window. A giant beanstalk had sprung up while he was sleeping, and it stretched up to the sky.

Jack ran outside and began to climb the beanstalk.

Up and up he went, higher

and higher, till he reached the top.

There he found a road,
which led to a big house.

Jack's tummy was rumbling with hunger, so he knocked on the large, wooden door.

A giant woman answered. She looked kind, and Jack asked if she would give him some breakfast.

"You will **BE** breakfast if my husband finds you!" she told Jack. "He's much bigger than me, and he eats children!"

But Jack begged and pleaded, and at last the woman let him in. She gave him some bread and milk, and hid him in a cupboard.

Soon Jack heard loud footsteps and felt the cupboard shake. The giant man was coming! Jack heard him roar,

"Fee-fi-fo-fum,

I smell the blood

of an Englishman!"

"Don't be so silly," the giant's wife said.
"You smell the sausages I've cooked for your
breakfast! Now sit down and eat."

After wolfing down three plates of sausages, the giant asked his wife to bring him his gold. She brought two big sacks filled with gold coins, which the giant began to count. But he was sleepy after his big breakfast and soon began to snore.

Jack crept out of the cupboard and grabbed one of the sacks. Then he rushed out of the house, along the road, and straight down the beanstalk.

Jack's mother was overjoyed to see him, and she was even happier when she saw the gold.

They lived well while the money lasted, but after a year, it had all been spent. Once again, Jack and his mother had nothing to eat.

"Don't worry, Mother," said Jack. "I'll just go back up the beanstalk to the giant's house."

And so he did. Just as before, Jack knocked on the door and begged the giant's wife for something to eat.

"Go away," she told him. "The last time you were here, a sack of gold disappeared. My husband was really cross!"

But once again, Jack begged and pleaded, and at last she let him in. She gave him some bread and milk and hid him in the cupboard.

Soon the giant stomped in, bellowing,

"Fee-fi-fo-fum,

I smell the blood of an Englishman!"

"Nonsense," said the giant's wife.
"You smell the yummy soup I've made
for your lunch."

Peeping through a crack in the cupboard door,
Jack saw the giant slurp down a big barrelful of soup,
and heard him tell his wife, "Bring me my hen!"

She put a fat red hen on the table, and the giant shouted,

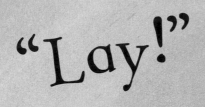

"Lay!"

To Jack's amazement, the hen laid a golden egg!

Jack waited until the giant was asleep.

Zzzzzzzz!

Then he jumped out and snatched the hen.
Fast as lightning, he dashed out of the house,

along the road ...

and

down

the

beanstalk.

Jack and his mother lived very well on the money they made from the hen's golden eggs. But Jack wanted to climb the beanstalk one last time.

He knew the giant's wife would not let him in again, so when she wasn't looking, he sneaked into the house and crawled into the cupboard.

Before long the giant came crashing in.

"Fee-fi-fo-fum, I smell the blood of an Englishman!"

he thundered.

"You smell the steaks I've cooked for your dinner," his wife said. And she put a platter of thick, juicy steaks in front of him.

After gobbling up the steaks, the giant took out a golden harp and said, **"Sing!"** The harp played a gentle lullaby, and soon the giant was fast asleep.

Jack sprang out, took the harp, and began to run. But the harp cried,

"Master! Master!"

... and the giant woke up.

With a roar, he leapt up and ran after Jack.

Holding the harp tightly, Jack ran for his life. As he scrambled down the beanstalk, he yelled,

"Mother! Mother! Bring the ax!"

Jack took the ax and started to chop down the beanstalk.

The giant quickly climbed back up to the top before it snapped in two.

That was the last time Jack saw him.

With the hen and the harp, Jack and his mother were able to live happily ever after—and they were never hungry again.

The End